DREAMT

A Book of Poetry

D.T. Caldwell

D Caldwell

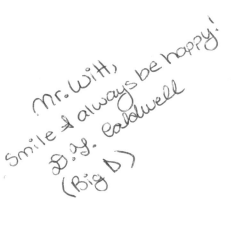

Mr. Witt,
Smile & always be happy!
D.J. Caldwell
(Big D)

CONTENTS

DREAMT:

A Book of Poetry

Written by:
D.T. Caldwell

Copyright © 2020 D.T. Caldwell
"Dreamt"

All rights reserved. No parts of this publication may be reproduced, distributed, or conveyed without express written permission from the author.

Published by:
D Caldwell

ACKNOWLEDGE-
MENTS

Thank you to the astonishing parents, grandparents, family, and friends in my life who have made the creation of these poems possible. Thank you to all of life's experiences that have aided in the inspiration to express these characters in the form of poetry. I am extraordinarily grateful to all who have touched my life both directly and indirectly. Any success of mine would not be possible, nor would it be as noteworthy, without your endless encouragement and love. Thank you all so much!

Poems, Cover, & Photographs by *D.T. Caldwell*

The destination might never be discovered, yet the **journey** will never be forgotten. If a **chance** is never taken, how will a **second chance** ever be bestowed? She **lost** herself in her wonderings of him and he with every breath she'd taken. It was only a matter of time before two disparate souls would be **one** step away.

Not a soul knew of the end he would remorse as he realized she had moved on now. Perhaps, their story would always be finer **written.** But in the end, **their closure** will be the words they never had spoken. Will it all be more than they had **dreamt?**

Enjoy this first glimpse into the nameless characters of the Series of Second Chances...

JOURNEY

The path will:
curve and wind,
jolt and vandalize,
sorrow and mourn,
as the day turns into a gloomy night.

But every destination is deserving of a long and difficult road,
one that will create:
memories and laughter,
lessons and solitude,
achievements and aspirations,
as the despairing dusk turns into a joyous dawn.

The route will be:
momentous and everlasting,
tiresome and heartbreaking,
rewarding and worthy,
yet the traveler will never forget the journey.

BROTHERHOOD

In the stars, the moon shines brightly,
illuminating the field below for all to see,
one last time.

The pride, the effort, the challenge,
the dedication, the loyalty, the joy, the despair,
the blood, the sweat, & the tears.

All come forth,
in the game,
one last time.

When the cheers silence, the band fades,
the shouting softens, & the lights dim,
it immobilizes like a tidal wave.

The intensity dwindles as the time draws near,
realization strikes,
it's like a bullet to the heart.

Strength is not without weakness,
tears of honor, sorrow, & elation are present,
one last time.

The boys of fall know what's coming,
they have waited for this moment,
never imagining it would appear.

They share the field,
fighting for the name embroidered on the front of their jerseys,
one last time.

ROGUE

She would run away,
pursuing the dreams she had dreamt at night,
chasing him into the setting sun,
rebelling against all odds.

She was a runaway,
birthing a light never before seen,
hoping for a reunion in time,
disobeying all advice.

Her creations would turn,
destined to follow the path hereby her footsteps,
destined to be marked in red,
destined to turn rogue.

CHANCE

A risk,
or a challenge.
A second opportunity,
or a moment of reconsideration.
An aspiration,
or an alluring entity.
How will you ever know what could have been?
Take a chance.

A WONDER & A MYSTERY

You were a wonder:
A symbol of pride,
A beacon of intensity,
A boy caught in the darkness.

I was a mystery:
An emblem of hope,
A signal of kindness,
A girl with a lantern in the darkness.

A wonder and a mystery.

ONE

One road away,
She lies there waiting for him,
Hoping,
Wishing and,
Dreaming of him being one road away.

It has all played out before her eyes,
A step was braved,
Moment by moment,
Day by day,
He inches closer to her until he's one turn away.

She can see him standing there,
Contemplating a move,
One that would bring him closer to her,
Aspiring and,
Intending her to be one door away.

He can see her standing there,
Dreaming of him being a door away,
Wondering if it will happen at all,
That's why she's there,
She's one step away.

One step away,
Will he take it?
Hopes and aspirations,
Dreams and intentions,
Have led them one road, one turn, one door, and *one* step away.

FEARBOUND

The sunlight brightens all around her,
the wild spring air coldly blows.
Though, the sunlight seems to darken into a tunnel,
creating a zone,
and the wind dies down until it stands still.

The pressure weighing heavily on her shoulders gets brushed off.
She is in her own time up high in that tower,
overwhelmed with emotion and cannot leap.

The stadium lights brighten all around him,
the delicate autumn breeze crisply blows.
Though, the stadium lights seem to darken,
highlighting only the endzone,
and the wind dies down until it stands still.

The pressure weighing heavily on his shoulders gets brushed off.
He is in his own time on that fifty-yard line,
overwhelmed with emotion and cannot run.

But they are not *fearbound.*

POSSIBLE

How is it possible?
You look at me like I'm the only girl in the room,
the only girl in your dreams,
the only girl in the world,
the only girl for you,
and in that moment, I am.
How is it possible?

FOOTBALL

First, you looked me in the eyes & I was mesmerized.

On that night, I had never dreamt of you & me.

On that night, I had never dreamt it possible.

The crowd roaring and the players shouting all faded away.

But little did we know...

All we needed was a single word, hello.

Likelihood of you & me went from zero to seven hundred.

Like we never dreamt before, now you &

me are possibly meant to be.

FOOTPRINTS

October had fallen upon them within a blink of an eye,
bringing the hint of November's chill
and unforgettable moments.

For the boys walked the field of battle one last time,
and she shed her tears in silence for them all
as she stood there hiding her pain.

Until all gathered together walking off,
in fifty and two disparate directions
leaving behind, on the field, their footprints.

ALWAYS THERE

YOU WERE-
Even if the cold air pushes away the warmth,
If all the hope is lost.
Even when the lights went dark,
when the stars were hidden behind the mist.
Even if we're horror-stricken,
If we're paralyzed by each other's smile.
Even when I turn the other way,
when I can't see what I had right in front of me.
-ALWAYS THERE.

ONLY

We inhale, we exhale
We don't have to aggravate,
We will let it be gradual, as
We inhale, we exhale.

I don't need an autograph,
I don't care about your politics,
I only want you,
I only...

You are grateful for what you have,
You don't categorize,
You only need me,
You only...

Do you remember the first time?
Do you recall when our gazes crossed?
Do you think of our hands brushing by?
Do you remember?

We inhale, we exhale
We don't aggravate,
We will always let it be gradual, as
We inhale, we exhale.

TELL ME

Tell me:
Do you want me as much as I want you?
Do you need me as much as I need you?
Tell me:
Has it all just been a game?
Has it all just been a figment of my mind?
Tell me:
Are you thinking of me when you lie awake at night?
Are you dreaming of me when your eyes finally slide closed?
Tell me:
Were you wishing it was me on your arm that night?
Were you fantasizing holding me waltzing that night?
Tell me:
Is there something worth fighting for?
Is there a chance that you and I can be?
Tell me:
Can we take each other by the hand and hold on tight?
Can we have this dance?
Tell me:
Do you want me as much as I want you?
Do you need me as much as I need you?

LOST

Lost
with every breath you've taken,
every move you've made.

Lost
feeling the touch of your hand,
the beat of your heart.

Lost
in this moment in time,
this winding road.

Lost
every breath,
every move.

Lost

WHY DON'T I?

Courageous,
That's what they always say:
You're courageous for going your own way,
but they don't know.

Every time I look at you,
I don't let my guard fall,
I don't throw my heart your way.

So why don't I want to close my eyes?
Why don't I want to look away?
Every time I look at you,
Why don't I?

EDGE

Wind in our hair like magic,
the chilled air turning from autumn to winter,
only two choices: flee or leap.

The view is mesmerizing,
It gives our smile and takes our breath,
our toes against the verge for awhile now.

To flee is to lose the sight,
to leap is to forever hold on,
two options, two people.

Affright and spellbound,
smiling with no breath,
we stand on the edge.

NAMELESS

We're nameless,
hiding from the crowd,
always on each other's minds,
stealing glances,
hoping no one sees.

We just can't look away,
we're nameless,
always letting curiosity overpower,
where is she, where is he,
this is more than we can muster.

We share a smile,
sending the other to their knees,
we're nameless,
as we find our breath caught,
oblivious to what surrounds.

We reveal our voices with a single word,
who knew it could mean so much,
who knew it would make us feel this way,
we're nameless,
praying we'll pick each other out in the crowd.

We walk shoulder to shoulder,
side by side,
exchanging our first words,
conversing alone as we look into each other's eyes,

we're nameless.

WOULD YOU?

If he knew...
of her guarded heart,
of her fear of failure and heartbreaks,
of a single thought dancing through her mind.
If you knew,
would you take my hand?
If she knew...
of his insecurities,
of his racing thoughts and pounding heart,
of a single hope dancing through his mind.
If you knew,
would you hold onto me?
If he knew...
she had no idea what to do,
she tried everything that scared her,
she wants him holding onto her.
If you knew,
would you stay?
If she knew...
he had never felt this way before,
he tried and tried and tried,
he wants her in his arms.
If you knew,
would you?

HERE

Here:
where the world won't seem so big,
where the birds sing their early morning songs.
Here:
where one does not only have to dream.
Here:
where the light will always shine true,
where the moon will cast its beam upon us.
Here:
where one can dance beneath the stars.
Here:
where love spreads infectiously,
where hope overpowers.
Here:
where our home lies.
Here:
where two people build a new beginning,
where memories are made.
Here:
where life begins and love never expires.
Here:
where our world revolves,
where each of life's chapters unravel.
Here:
where we are meant to be.

HOPE

Have you ever lost yourself in your thoughts? Of him? Of her?
It's like nothing they've ever felt before. It's bright and it's new,
blossoming in his and in her soul.

On a night like tonight, he can dream of her and she of him.
And it's like he can reach for her arm and she can feel the tips of his
fingers upon her skin.

Please, don't give up. Hold on to what you have, but

don't be afraid to take a step. He engulfs her in his

arms, and she rests her head on his shoulder.

Eventually, he will be hers and she will be his.

BELIEVE

Help me to see,
the light shining through the dark,
the sterling emotions cascading by,
the meaning of it all,
help make me believe.

I still can't believe it,
my back to the room,
blocking out the sunlight;
Help me to see,
help make me believe.

How can it be?
What if it is possible?
Will I have to trust?
Help me to see,
help make me believe.

I won't ever believe it,
the wonder glistening in the brown of his eyes,
the catching of his breath at a single glance;
Help me to see,
help make me believe.

INTENSE

The delicate movement of his fingers and his cautious hand that reaches out as the sunlight reveals his shadow.

Her knees grow weak.

His voice lowered to a mere whisper as he speaks softly into her ear, her hair blowing from his gentle breath, as he leans in until his lips are nearer.

Her eyes go unblinking.

The tips of his fingers slide gently across her knuckles, barely felt until he gives her an infectious smile to fill the void of silence.

Her breath catches in her chest.

His gaze, transfixed upon her from across the room, unable to break away, and seeking her out in a sea of a thousand faces.

Her heart flutters to a stop.

His stare, polluted with inexpressible emotion never before witnessed by mankind, only written for a fictional character in a novel.

Her soul forever locks onto that of his.

But above all else, his reposeful movements, his alluring vocals, his heartfelt touch, and his vehement gaze all are and always will be so unexpectedly

INTENSE.

DREAMT

Your gaze from across the room,
Your smile that brightens the night,
Your intensity.

It's more than I ever thought possible,
More than I had imagined,
More than I had dreamt.

My holding of your gazes,
My grabbing of your attention,
My hope.

It's more than I ever thought possible,
More than I had imagined,
More than I had dreamt.

Your consistent courtesies,
Your spontaneous waves of greeting,
Your widening smile.

It's more than just a friend,
More than only a coincidence,
More than I had dreamt.

My willingness to open up,
My observations of you,
My brightening hopes.

It's more than just a friend,
More than only a coincidence,
More than I had dreamt.

You had me from the moment you first looked into my eyes,
I had you from the moment I revealed my voice,
We caught one another.

It's more than we ever thought possible,
More than we had imagined,
More than we had **dreamt.**

PEEK

The days,
once unnumbered,
had
reached the
unexpected.

Within moments,
the hours
had
approached their
peak.

But he
only now
had
seen the
time.

He saw
what he
had
causing him
panic.

The boy
noticed she
had
moved on
now.

He knew
now he
had
his last
peek.

HAD

The past is in the past,
moments in time that cannot be remade,
history upon a page written in immutable ink.

She was at the tips of his fingers,
heart fluttering at the sound of his name,
eyes brightening upon a single glance.

He was standing merely a step away,
mind racing with a thousand unvoiced words,
smile broadening across his face.

But his feasibility was swept from beneath him,
feet trembling as if standing upon a rug,
body leaning until he fell.

Down on his knees with his hands clasped so tight,
pleading for her unwarranted forgiveness,
wishing for her to grant him a second chance.

The boy knew of his loathsome mistakes,
anguish merging to the surface,
chest aching from a heartbreak.

What if he had seen it from the start,
tantalized with truth behind his movement,
known all along what he had?

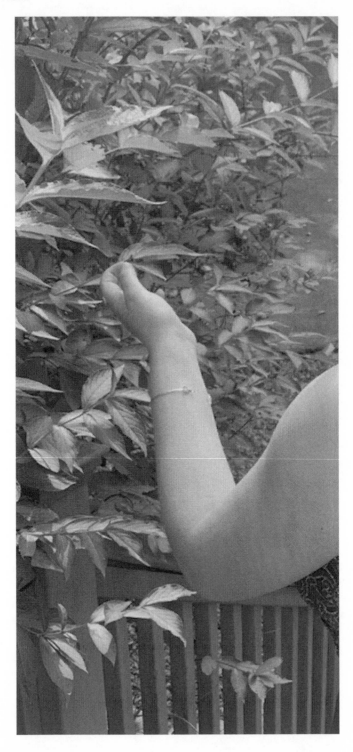

SHOULD'VE BEEN

He should've been chasing her,
She should've been sitting back,
We should've been.

He should've been trying too,
She should've been reaching out her hand,
We should've been.

They should've been the light in the dark,
They should've been dancing beneath the stars,
They should've been more.

He should've been doing everything possible,
She should've been beaming with joy,
We should've been.

He should've been taking her hand,
She should've been in his arms,
We should've been.

THE LIGHT

The city had yielded to the dark,
streetlights dimming more each night,
beings going around with no remark,
but then there was the light.

He gazed upon the lights shining overhead,
fantasizing his final minutes of a lost second chance,
once he saw her, his heart filled with dread,
he had dreamt of seeing her again.

He had once been revered,
the warriors defending the pride,
hoping the end would be adhered,
but they would succumb to war.

The lights went out long ago,
streetlights gradually burning out,
the city had fallen to the dark,
but then there was *the light*.

FORGET...

Two paths opened in the distance,
destination unknown.
He went one way and she another,
discovering purpose.

The crossing was crowded as ever,
conveying memories.
She picked him out within minutes,
conducting emotions.

The roads met at long last,
merging fates.
He locked his eyes on her within moments,
mesmerizing recollections.

Two unconnected avenues proceeded,
forlorn kismet.
She could stall in her years henceforth,
forget him.

Two disparate choices become relevant,
foregoing fate.
He could never in all his years hereafter,
forget her.

As the pathway winds on,
forcing change.
They could not ever erase the past,
forget...

UNTANGLE

Brown eyes met blue for the first time,
it was prominent and so intense,
guiding him and her into a new light.

The fear overtook.
The clock spun on,
it was steady and so fast,
telling him and her to take a step forth.
But the hours ran short.

Hurt was inescapable,
it was heart-rending and loathsome,
piercing him and her in the soul.
She valiantly faded from his life.

A second chance had lapsed,
it was tender and slanted,
pulling him and her apart.
He was stranded alone.

Brown eyes met blue for the last time,
it was crestfallen and so fervid,
guiding him and her into a new light.
Until the memories *untangle.*

I'LL WAIT

I'll wait.

For the nervous energy coursing through me,
For the constant signs that lead me to you,
For the giddy, uncontrollable happiness.
For you,

I'll wait.
For the heart-stopping smiles,
For the melting, unbreakable gazes,
For the unnecessary, reliable courtesies.
For you,

I'll wait.
For the dances to not only be imagined,
For the embrace to be more than merely a daydream,
For the companionship to blossom to life.
For you,

I'll wait.

WAKE

All those moments seemed like a fantasy,
coming true only in the hours of the dark.
A mystifying figure stands on the horizon,
reaching delicate fingers nearer.

You stand so still till her fingertips are merely an inch away,
aching to feel her heavenly touch.
But then eyelids flutter,
and you wake.

You stand so still till she feels the static
of your mesmerizing hair,
fancying to have the strands between her poised fingers.
But then blue eyes go uncovered,
and she wakes.

If only you had seen with your eyes,
making your dreams true to life.
She could only hope that you would see,
stirring from your endless slumber.

Every night has an authentic dawn,
depicting the struggles and destinies.
You should have acted when she bestowed your second chance,
possibly you would not be left in her *wake*.

CLOSES HER DOOR

The rain pelts down,
a thousand droplets strike the earth
as if they were knives,
drowning the boy and the girl
in the sorrow of the beckoning night.

Her door had been cracked open,
the bright light sneaking out
to give him hope,
sparking his desires to come
ever so nearer to her.

His eyes widened at the sight,
heart pounding within the strength of his chest
as the fear overshadowed,
allowing him to step inside her
once closed door.

In a blink of his brown eyes,
a thousand knives pierce him in the heart
as autumn drew to a close,
engulfing him in an intense feeling
of his own remorse.

Give her one final chance,
a dance on the edge of the world
that only ends with a fall,
his heart breaking to pieces
as she closes her door.

The sun seeps out from behind the storm,
a thousand rays beat upon the earth
as if they were faith,
devouring the boy and the girl
in the delirium of the enticing morn.

ONE LAST GLANCE

She had always been beside him,
standing there even in the darkest hour,
and he never thought she would walk.

His touch was so benign,
trailing his fingertips across her demure knuckles,
and he never thought time could expire.

She showed him her back,
walking away from the hurt and despair,
and she never thought he would follow.

His gaze was infectiously intense,
refusing to look away from her eyes,
and he never thought she could withstand.

Neither prepared for the dawn,
struggling to accept the inevitable fate awaiting,
and never thought they would take their one last glance.

TWO

Two hours had expired
from the first moment he and she met.
She replayed the intensity of his brown eyes
gazing into her meek blue.
She could only think in two weeks,
his curiosity would peak.

Two weeks flew by
from the first moment he and she met.
In a sea of a million untold faces,
he never ceased to find his mystery girl.
She could only think in two months,
his attentiveness would fall.

Two months passed
from the first moment he and she met.
He had her in the forefront of his mind,
protecting her from all which lurked.
She could only think in two years,
his heed would crash.

Two years had expired
from the first moment he and she met.
She replayed the intensity of his brown eyes
gazing into her wild blue.
She could never think in two years,
his curiosity would be *tireless*.

NOT A SOUL

She was the adventurous and she was the inspiration,
caring and lighthearted,
resolute and humorous,
not a soul aware of her name.
But then there was him.

He was the pride and he was the joy,
wondrous and strong,
revered and idolized,
not a soul unaware of his title.
But then there was her.

She had him at the tips of her fingers,
it merely took her fidelity,
she had him in the palm of her hand,
for she let fall her wild voice.
Who would have thought?

He had her at the tips of his fingers,
it only took his spellbinding smile,
he had her in the palm of his hand,
for he let fall his impassioned gaze.
Who would have believed?

She was the intrepid and he was the dignity,
the considerate and he the miraculous,
the undaunted and he the star,
not a soul unaware of their bond.
Yet the end he would remorse.

BLINDED

The darkness overpowers,
she spins,
around and around,
with no end,
none in sight.

Yet she marches on,
blinded,
blinded by the night,
blinded by the fright,
blinded by him.

Soon the light overwhelms,
burning the ground,
blocking her sight,
she can't see,
not anymore.

His hand over her eyes,
guiding her,
encouraging her
through the brightness,
or so she had thought.

One day,
the darkness will brighten,
the light will dim,
she'll find what's real,
waiting for her while she had been *blinded.*

CROSSROAD

One step forth, no stepping back,
There are two directions on the horizon:
North or South.

North;
burnished and level the road remains,
providing a facile, kind route.

South;
rugged and boisterous the trail lingers,
granting an adventurous, winding route.

North or South?
Furbished or precipitous?
She stands at a crossroad.

WILL

What will you see?
When you close your eyes,
when the lights burn out,
when the clouds roll across the sky,
and the rain pours down,
will you dream of me?

What will you do?
If the snow grows deep,
if your bank runs low,
if this life succumbs to darkness,
and all turns against you,
will you wish for me?

What will you ponder?
Once the bad overpowers the good,
once there is nothing left,
once there is only the two of us,
and everything has gone,
will you imagine me?

What will you seek?
Presuming that the stars are shining,
presuming that the moment has come,
presuming that you are prepared,
and I am standing in the distance,
will you reach for me?

What will you believe?
Whether you dream,
whether you wish,
whether you imagine,
and reach,
will you hope for me?

WORTH

Is it worth it?
Worth my time?
My happiness?
My hope?
My beliefs?
My efforts?
Is it worth it?

He put our story on replay,
his smile brightened the late hour,
his fingertips brushed against my own,
his attempts bring forth more and more hope,
he put our story on replay.

The disk spins 'round and 'round,
like there's no end in sight,
It just plays the same scene over and over,
on and on,
on and on.

We're caught in a web,
It's strangling us,
keeping you from me and me from you,
we know we have to break it,
but what will you do?

Is it worth it?
Worth my time?
My happiness?
My hope?
My beliefs?
My efforts?
Are you *worth* it?

PROMISE

You'll know what you have before it's gone,
promise?
You'll be there in the moonlight,
promise?
Your hand will engulf my small fingers,
promise?

Promise?
On a night just like tonight, you'll hold on,
as if all you had could up and fly away,
and you'll know what you have before it's gone,
promise?

If the lights are shining down,
brighter than the stars above,
you'll be there in the moonlight,
ready for a dance,
promise?

When the darkness surrounds,
choking out the hope in all the world,
your hand will engulf my small fingers,
and you will plant your roots right beside me,
promise?

Each day will be an adventure,
one worth living for,
the days will go by fast and the years slow,
and this life will be something to remember,

promise?

There will be triumphs and failures,
dreams and nightmares,
aspirations and aimlessness,
and there will be you,
promise?

You'll know what you have before it's gone,
promise!
You'll be there in the moonlight,
promise!
Your hand will engulf mine,
promise!

ASHES

A single spark lights a fire,
one which burns passionately through the dark.
It glows brighter and brighter by the day,
blotting out what stands on the horizon.
But, in time, every flame must dim.
A small flicker gives one last glimmer,
until blackness surrounds.
What has gone astray in the fire
is found in the remains.
Who ever knew what could be found
in the ashes?

SECOND CHANCE

Darkness will fall,
sweeping away all hope.
You will get lost,
never to be found.
Light will be at the end,
waiting for the arrival.
Just keep moving forth,
earn your second chance.

WHAT IF?

What if
he had not been paralyzed with fear
and made her walk out of his life for a while,
she had not been wary of him when her eyes
first laid upon,
he had seen with his eyes and not his
fantasies,
she had believed him bona fide from the start,
he had not raised her so high he was unable to
reach,
she had not taken him for who he truly was
deep within his heart and his soul,
&
he had known all along what he had in the
palm of his hand before she was gone?
What if?

APPREHEND

The moment his eyes locked onto hers,
                                  he was entranced,
searching for her with every wind in the
                                  road,
dreaming of her when the stars filled the night
                                  sky.
She was more than he could fathom.

The instant his brown eyes met hers,
                                  she was uncertain,
not knowing why, he searched for her with every curve in the
                                  road,
dreaming of her when the stars revealed themselves in the dark
                                  sky.
He was more than she could grasp.

The boy had an unexpected intensity,
gazing inexplicably up at her in her tower no matter the
                                  day,
refusing to relent until he found what he was
                                  inquiring.
She was more than he could unravel.

The girl was an unsolved mystery,
losing the breath in her lungs upon falling to his content
                                  stare,
walking into the distance without looking over her shoulder at
him

one final time.
He was more than she could ever discern.

The days flew by in a blink of an eye,
sharing no words between the unsettled
pair,
seeming as if no time had passed from the moment he saw her
standing across the road.
She was more than he could ever *apprehend*.

BARS

Every breath.

He stands before her own two eyes,
his smile melted her and trapped her there.
Her aspirations led her down a darkened hall,
her hope brightened him and held him there.

Every momentous exchange.

He inches closer with every passing moment,
his gaze intense and smitten.
She courageously reached out,
her stare gentle and mysterious.

Every move.

He needs her in his arms,
desiring to hold her so tight.
She wanted him to hold her,
dreamt of being in his arms so tight.

Every kindhearted touch.

But the steel rods divide them,
blocking them from being together.
He thinks he needs her, and she thought she wanted him,
they are separated by bars.

ONLY A DANCE

The stars shone in the hours of darkness,
days polluted with tempests and fear,
thoughts of one moment erasing years of pain,
he held his hand out to her.

The moonlight veiled behind a shadow,
days tainted with squalls and trepidation,
thoughts of one moment imprinting years of pain,
she reached for his hand.

Holding her in his arms against the strength of his chest,
breaths colliding as the heavenly bodies shone above,
thoughts of one moment and years of pain,
they could share a dance.

Feeling his arms wrapped around her waist,
eyes glistening at the sight of the other,
thoughts of one moment enticing years of pain,
they could share only a dance.

UNFINISHED

Time was ripped out from beneath our feet as if it were a rug,
you collapsed one way and I another. We began so quietly in
the comfort of the other's eyes, but the single spark produced
a flame for all to see. The crackling of the fire was known to all,
like fireworks spreading across the star-filled sky. But time was
ripped out from beneath our feet as if it were a rug, you collapsed
one way and I another. It was never meant to be this way, yet was
it ever in the palm of our hands? We were destined to go unfin.....

WRITTEN

His gaze is like a vow,
promising her that he'll take her in his arms.
But his unspoken words are broken,
never meaning to amend their inevitable plight.
On a sheet of paper locked away in a vault,
their story will always be finer written.

FADED

In a blink of his brown eyes,
all he had known was stolen,
He never saw it coming.
all he had desired up and walked,
He should have never crushed her spirits.
all he had dreamt suddenly faded away.
Looking back, he will always remorse.

In a bat of his untold gray eyes,
everything he had thought was wrong,
He never thought what could have been.
everything he had fought hard for was gone,
He should have never left her in the dust.
everything he had dreamt of at night faded away.
Looking back, he will always miss.

In a twinkling of his blue eyes,
all he had wished for began to come true,
He never thought she felt the same.
all he had learned gave way to his advance,
He should have walked alongside her sooner.
all he had thought impossible suddenly faded to the forefront.
Looking back, he will always smile.

HOW?

How did she not see it?
It had been there from the beginning,
all the signs pointing to it.
Yet her eyes went unseeing.

When did it all happen?
His hand upon her back guiding her forth,
every last day.
Yet her timeline went obscured.

Had he been waiting all along?
Sitting back in the shadows to observe her,
since the fall.
Yet her blind smile went faultless.

Why had she not felt it?
The nervous energy coursing through her veins,
ever since he smirked.
Yet her mind went blank.

How did she not see him?
He had been there from the beginning,
all the signs pointing to him.
Yet her eyes went unseeing... until now.

PATIENTLY

He slowly crept into her life,
showed her there's nothing to fear
and much to discover.
Long has he awaited,
serenely.

Day by day, he got her to reveal her voice,
encouraged her to open up little by little
and she didn't even realize.
Long has he awaited,
considerately.

Sunlight turned to moonlight, he inched nearer,
let her know that he was there
and she leaned in.
Long has he awaited,
quietly.

Before she knew, he called her a good friend,
overcame his nerves to stand by her side
and she knew he didn't have to be.
Long has he awaited,
diligently.

He slowly crept, crept into her life,
showed her there was nothing to fear
and so much to discover.
Long has he and long has she awaited,

patiently.

SMILE

She lost herself in his smirk,
capturing her breath,
tempering the beat of her heart.

He went adrift in her brightening grin,
pilfering the words off his tongue,
meddling with the placement of his steps.

She and he forfeited themselves,
omitting the thought of averting the eyes,
cherishing each other's **smile.**

VAULT

A locked box is surrounded by a thousand bricks,
protecting her from all the hurt,
saving her from the past,
leading her to safety,
keeping her away.

There is a crease in the rigidity of her blockade,
giving him a chance,
putting herself on the line,
praying he can break through,
hoping he is meant to be.

Do not be afraid of what lies behind the wall,
a hopeful smile on the darkest nights,
a hand so desperate to hold another,
a challenge like no other,
a *vault* holding her heart.

JUST

You don't have to be afraid,
of failure,
of rejection,
of her.
She's *just* a girl.

And you don't have to worry,
about disapproval,
about heartbreak,
about him.
He's *just* a boy.

She's *just* a girl and he's *just* a boy,
two people,
taking a step closer,
and closer.
She's *just* a girl and he's *just* a boy.

WANT

The inspiration laying within his smile,
The genuineness of her touch,
The devotion of his kindness,
The compassion in her heart,
The variety of his temperament,
The wit on the tip of her tongue,
The integrity behind his words,
The fun in her laughter,
The dreams from his night,
The mystery of her measures,
The acceptance of his hand,
The warmth of her soul,
The patience in his steps;
It's all that he and she *WANT.*

FALLING

Standing at the cliff,
gazing down upon the disarray of the terrain.
She's five thousand feet high,
quivering in fright.
What if she falls,
falling through the air?

Never will she return to the cliff's edge,
seeing the astonishing view below.
She would be lying five thousand feet down,
hoping for a chance.
If she falls,
falling through the air.

She takes a breath,
releasing it slow.
A trembling foot stretches out,
touching only the passing breeze.
What if she falls,
falling through the air?

Will he catch her?
Hold her in his arms so tight?
Not thinking of letting her go?
What if she falls,
falling so hard?
Will he catch her?

Standing at the cliff,
gazing down at the beauty of the terrain.
She's five thousand feet high,
quivering in excitement.
She's FALLING,
FALLING through the air.

DOES HE?

Does he,
stare from across the room,
make it feel like you're the only two around even in a crowd,
become anxious whenever you're near,
lean in so close until his lips are merely
an inch away from your ear,
wait on the street for you to meet,
find a way to have his hand upon your skin,
hurry to reach you before it is too late,
run his fingers over your hair when it catches his eye,
care for your every whim,
stand by you, knowing of your insecure nature
and your guarded heart?
Does he?

OCEAN

Your crystal clear,
ocean blue eyes
sparkle in the sunlight.

There's a ripple
cascading back
into the horizon.

But there's a tide
rushing in,
dampening the sand.

The crystal blueness
of the wave
consumes me, all the while...

Your crystal clear,
ocean blue eyes
sparkle in the sunlight.

SEE

A million thoughts fog her mind,
spiraling and bringing her down.
She is lost on the inside,
never knowing which way to turn.
Never sees what's right in front of her eyes.

He is so close,
reaching his hand out to her.
It has been this way once before,
so close.
But her eyes were blocked by another's hand.

Open my eyes,
make me aware of what could be.
Take my hand in your hand,
guide me to where I need to be.
Be my eyes so I can see.

That boy will never falter,

always entrusting his own desires.
But does she see him standing there?
What about her haunting past?
Is this the dawn of a new light?

She is tired of falling,
exhausted by her heart melting and then shattering.
She will let fall her rainbow of colors,
a fierce bullet to her heart is history.
Now is his entrancing arrow.

Open my eyes,
make me aware of what could be.
Take my hand in your hand,
guide me to where I need to be.

Be my eyes so I will see.

HEART

She has fallen more times than she can count,
He has shattered more times than he can recall.
Both so scared.
He will have to catch her when she falls,
She will have to piece him back together when he shatters.

All the times she has ached for more,
All the times he has prayed for a good girl.
All the moments she has waited for,
All the moments he has wanted.
All entranced in a serene power,
All entranced in heart.

She has lost herself in her thoughts for hours,
He has found himself hiding for days.
Both so anxious.
He will have to ease her racing mind,
She will have to find a reason for him to step into the dawn.

All the times she has ached for more,
All the times he has prayed for a girl like her.
All the moments she has waited for him,
All the moments he has wanted.
All entranced in a serene power,
All entranced in heart.

She has been oblivious,
He has been slowly creeping closer.
Both so shy.

He will have to show her his intentions,
She will have to step in his direction.

All the times she has ached for him,
All the times he has prayed for her.
All the moments she has waited for him,
All the moments he has wanted with her.
All entranced in a serene power,
All entranced in heart.

FLUKE OR FATE

Was it a fluke?
The moments she and he shared:
conversations they had,
dreams they depicted,
and,
traits they partook.
The conversations they had:
nervous energy coursing through,
unexpected experiences,
and,
lullabies through the night.
The dreams they depicted:
love blossoming true,
tranquility for all,
and,
summer carrying the torch of hope.
The traits they partook:
relentless kindness cascading on,
ambitions which strengthen,
and,
family above all else.
It was fate.

EYES

Words, beautiful and unique,
give luminosity to the moment.

But phrases can go unvoiced,
depriving the heart and the soul.

Eyes, beautiful blue,
true to the person standing before.

What goes unsaid is perceptible,
laying within his eyes.

Look to him upon the silence that fills the air,
hear the words spoken with his eyes.

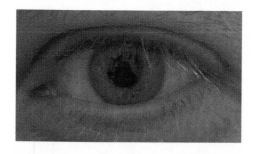

DAYDREAM

Blithesome blue eyes laid upon him
in the moments of light
with no whimsical stars twinkling overhead.

Wistful crystal eyes locked onto her
in the dawn of daylight
with no quaint stars shining above.

Shy crystal fell upon mischievous blue
to open both their eyes
with no fated destination in mind.

He kindhearted and she the devilish
lost in each other's eyes
with no notion of a daydream.

BREATH

His hand stretches out,
fingers unclenching gradually,
and he inhales a *breath*.

She stands still,
eyes locked on his reaching hand,
and she inhales a *breath*.

He wavers for a mere moment,
fingers hovering over her skin,
and he holds a *breath*.

She bites the corner of her rosy lips,
eyes transitioning to the floor,
and she holds a *breath*.

He closes the distance between,
fingers caressing her skin,
and he exhales a *breath*.

She relaxes her anxieties,
eyes meeting his gaze,
and she exhales a *breath*.

THEIR CLOSURE

All the moments they've shared,
Every vault.
All the laughs they've had,
Every remorse.
All the gazes they've held,
Every hurt.
All the smiles they've exchanged,
Every hopelessness.
All the feelings they've realized,
Every tear.
All the dreams they've dreamt,
Every heartache.
All the moments they've shared.

All in all, every last day comes to this,
her words escaping her lips,
his response shocking all
to move on with their lives and
truly hold another's hand.
All in all, every last day comes to this:
their closure.

HER LETTER

Her mind racing to and fro,
fantasizing an unknown conclusion,
until she wrote:

Dear You,

All I ask of you is this:
Why me?
The moment my eyes met your gaze,
my breath was caught.
You were so intense.
I knew you were more than I had dreamt.
Yet never did you help make me believe,
be my eyes so I will see.
You were a wonder and I was a mystery,
a beacon of intensity and a signal of kindness.
I was lost feeling the touch of your hand,
the beat of your heart.
All those moments seemed like a fantasy,
coming true only in the hours of dark.
Possibly on a sheet of paper locked away in a vault,
our story will always be finer written.
But, do not make this the end.
Do not make our story only a dance.
But if my words go unseen, forever remember this:
Our unfinished story was more than we had dreamt.

Sincerely,

Your once one & only

P.S.- please, don't be a stranger

HIS LETTER

The years scurried past,
causing her mind to go unrestful,
until he wrote:

Dear You,

You are the adventurous and you are the inspiration,
I was the pride and I was the joy,
but what for?
The end I would remorse.
I have never wished to make our story only a dance.
I only needed you and you only wanted me.
Still, I only need you.
Because you are a mystery.
Not a soul unaware of my title, except you.
And for you, I'll wait.
But if my words go unseen, forever remember me and this:
you were more than I had dreamt.

Thanks for thinking of me,
Your once one & only

P.S.- you won't ever be a stranger

ABOUT THE AUTHOR

Writing has always been and always will be an escape. It allows me to escape to a world of my choosing and immerse myself in it. Writing is a hobby to me because I relish it, so I never expected to be sharing it. Thank you for reading my work and I hope you enjoy it!

I am a sports enthusiast. Baseball and softball have always been my favorites. However, I recently learned that football and wrestling are entertaining to experience. My love for sports has made me realize that I wish to enter the field of medicine in the future while, of course, writing on the side. Please, everyone, keep reading and always be happy!

D.T. Caldwell

COMING SOON...

SYNOPSIS OF *SØREN*

a conflicted captain

a love-struck soldier,
a hoodlum law woman

a free-spirited pilot
a screwball mechanic

a turncoat doctor

a yearning passenger
a mysterious dancer

a tormented prisoner

Nine people with nine intricate personalities, disparate occupations, prominent skills, and soul-stirring pasts are offered a heaven-sent chance. A chance to transform their imprudent lives into something worth remembering. Nevertheless, the charmed opportunity is not free. It must be earned.

In the year 3755, the travelers and crew of personal spacecraft *Fortuna* must exploit their predestined strengths and their inevitable weaknesses to overcome their greatest calamity. One job has the ability to change their lives yet bring each of them face to face with their most taunting fears. Their only hope is in each other. But can a conflicted captain, a love-struck soldier, a hoodlum law woman, a free-spirited pilot, a screwball mechanic, a turncoat doctor, a yearning passenger, a mysterious dancer, and a tormented prisoner be trusted?

A FIRST LOOK INTO *SØREN*

...Security Feed: Brig...

A boy who had conditioned muscles hidden beneath his t-shirt with his longer, dark brown hair sticking out in multiple directions, laid on his side on the filthy, hard floor as his eyelids began to flutter. His eyebrows went upwards and then downwards as he inhaled a breath soundlessly. The boy trailed his fingers, which were cuffed behind his back with a high-tech device, along the metal floor that was aberrantly cold to the touch. At last, he opened his eyes to see the woman clad in all black with hair the color of the darkest ash standing over him.

The woman stood with one hand on her hip which were spread shoulder width apart while holding a black baton in her free hand. She had a metallic black belt around her small waist that was lined with bullets and a holster holding her pistol upon her hip. She tapped her foot covered in black leather on the ground rhythmically to the beat of her calm heart. The woman observed the boy look up at her upon returning to consciousness to reveal his expressionless face.

Without further hesitation, the boy smirked at her with a slight chuckle lacking the accustomed smile, "Am I supposed to be intimidated, Kirsten?" Though his hair was sticking out in every direction known to man, the front of it was clinging to his forehead from a cold sweat. "Scaring someone who has nothing to lose," his complexion was paler than he had been moments prior, "isn't worth the time."

"Scaring you?" Kirsten folded her arms across her chest as she walked around the boy in circles, continuing her attempt to intimidate him, "I've been in this business for a long time." She placed her foot on the boy's leg, stepping her full weight onto him rather than going around him completely. "It doesn't matter who you think you are," she bent forward at the waist and whispered in his ear as she was situated behind him, "you will be scared."

"Oh, I'm petrified," he grumbled under his breath as he shifted around and brought his knee up higher as he began to get feeling back in his lower extremities. He recognized that he had been shot with a weapon meant to both shock him and knock him unconscious. He had experienced it in previous years, and he knew that moving was the only way to keep his muscles from tensing harshly within twelve hours.

The woman noticed the boy's movements immediately and kicked him in the thigh to ram his leg against the metal floor, inflicting pain upon him, "I didn't permit you to move." She pressed her weight into his leg as she stood on him slightly as she had done moments prior. "You move when I tell you to move," she whacked him with the black baton on the side of his arm, causing it to turn red instantly, and she spat his name, "Søren."

"A woman with no badge and no work for years," he looked her in the eyes fearlessly, "is bound for more trouble than good." He sat up slightly to be closer to her, ignoring the discomfort of her thick, leather boot on his leg, "Kirsten Xavier."

In anger, the woman brought her leg back and rammed the point of her toe into the boy's side with all of her might. He immediately rolled over onto his side as he wheezed quietly for breath from the pain shooting through his body. He bit his lower lip to keep from crying out as the woman slammed the cell door behind her and climbed the ladder up to the main level, leaving him by his lonesome.

The moment the boy knew that the woman was well out of earshot, he released a pain-filled moan as he closed his eyes and rested his head against the coolness of the floor. He scooted himself back against the wall to be hiding in the shadows of the already darkened room and took deep breaths to control the pain in his side. He twisted onto his stomach slightly as he pressed his forehead against the cold floor, relieved by the coolness as he waited for the next step in the interrogation.

...End-Security Feed: Brig...

The woman who had brown-hair that was braided off to the side with strands hanging over her face to hide her features, sat in the pilot's seat to observe the live footage from the camera in the brig. Her jaw was remarkably tense as she observed the abusive behavior of Kirsten Xavier towards the prisoner. Although he was a prisoner, she did not believe the members of her crew had the right to treat another individual in such a manner and that included herself. Each of them had made their mistakes and each of them should be granted a chance to change their impudent lives for the better.

She got herself to her feet and left the cockpit without saying a word. However, the man who sat in the copilot's seat leapt to his feet to chase after the woman as he attempted to wrap his brain around the situation. He grasped onto the woman's bicep gently, yet firmly, "Hold on."

"Ranger?" The woman, the captain of the ship, turned to face the man, her second-in-command. Her gaze was unexpectedly intense and utterly determined as she had made up her mind.

The man licked his dry lips nervously at her angered, frustrated gaze and he chose to speak in a soft voice to not infuriate her further, "He knew her name, Eden." He lowered his voice as he thought of all the moments the woman had shared pieces of her past with him and forced him to put them together until he came to a conclusion of his own, "Are you ready for your past to catch up with you?"

SYNOPSIS OF *ROGUE*

It began with a shadow.
A shadow which emerged through the mystical fog.
The owner of said shadow was oblivious to the fate
which lied in the filth of what lurked on the horizon.
Could the military brat destined to turn rogue be the hero?
The hero of which the city of second
chances had long been awaiting?
It *all* began with a shadow.

A FIRST LOOK
INTO ROGUE

A shadow emerged through the mystical fog settling within the base of the city and it swept into the alley formed by the two skyscrapers. A girl with straight, black hair containing red highlights throughout, hastily thrown into a ponytail with loose strands hanging by the sides of her face, was the owner of said shadow. Meanwhile, a unit of men dressed in military uniforms came bursting through the fog after the girl with their weapons in hand, prepared to fire should the order be given by their General.

At that time, the girl came to the side of a building made purely of cement, acting as a barrier between her and freedom. She whirled around making her stunning hair fly until it landed on her opposite shoulder and her breath was caught momentarily at the sight of the men behind her. A single spotlight struck across the girl's face revealing her features for the first time due to the darkness that had once surrounded her. She was average height for a girl of her age with a curvy build which revealed her athleticism and her slender body displayed the lack of nutrition she received. She wore a tight black tank top that was torn just above her belly button to show off skin beneath an oversized, unbuttoned, red flannel shirt with a tear in the sleeve to reveal her bruised shoulder. A pair of baggy, black cargo pants and aged Converse sneakers finished her attire. Most notably, the girl had Cal Ripken blue eyes filled with mischief and a level of proudness that no single soul, not even herself, would ever understand.

A man with a silver handlebar mustache, dressed in proper

military apparel strode through the surrounding soldiers who had gotten themselves into proper position, aiming their weapons at the girl. Thus, there were eighteen red laser dots lining the length of the girl's body, threatening to pierce her with the awaiting bullet. The sight of a single red laser from the barrel of a gun was enough to send a veteran soldier into a panicked state. However, the girl simply lifted her arm out to the side, gracefully waving her fingers to create a stunning light show. The girl's actions caused the man with the handlebar mustache to stop in his tracks, scuff his military issued boot against the pavement, and place his hands on his hips to glare at her.

The girl simply lowered her arm to dangle by her hip, clenching her hand into a fist, and widening her stance to be shoulder width apart. Meanwhile, her eyes darkened with danger, anger, and a sense of absurd fearlessness.

After what felt like hours of maintaining a staring contest, the man with the silver handlebar mustache removed his customized pistol from his holster and he dropped his arm to the side. He smirked evilly and gestured to the concrete buildings situated around them and his armed, highly trained soldiers, "You've got nowhere to go, Girl!"

There wasn't a moment's hesitation on her end of the line, "Never have."

*Who are the characters embedded within
the poems of Dreamt: A Book of Poetry?*

*Read the upcoming Series of Second
Chances to find out!*

THANKS FOR READING!

-D.T. Caldwell

Made in the USA
Middletown, DE
09 July 2020

12282263R00071